THE
HAPPY
PRINCE

INTERNATIONAL AWARD FOR ILLUSTRATION
PREMIO INTERNAZIONALE D'ILLUSTRAZIONE
PREMIO INTERNACIONAL DE ILUSTRACIÓN

On 30 March 2015, the jury of the 6th International Award for
Illustration at the Bologna Children's Book Fair, comprising
Anna Castagnoli, Martin Salisbury and Teresa Tellechea, and
supported by the Fundación SM, unanimously chose to grant
the award to Maisie Paradise Shearring (born 1991, Hull, UK).

The prize included the Spanish publication of this book, specially
commissioned from the illustrator after she received the award.

To Susan and John, for always being there.

First published in the United Kingdom in 2017 by
Thames & Hudson Ltd, 181A High Holborn, London WC1V 7QX

www.thamesandhudson.com

This paperback edition first published in 2018

First published in 2017 in the United States of America by
Thames & Hudson Inc., 500 Fifth Avenue, New York, New York 10110

www.thamesandhudsonusa.com

Original edition © 2016 Ediciones SM
Illustrations and adapted text © 2016 Maisie Paradise Shearring
This edition © 2017 Thames & Hudson Ltd, London

British Library Cataloguing-in-Publication Data
A catalogue record for this book is available from the British Library

Library of Congress Control Number 2016961553

ISBN: 978-0-500-65155-1

Printed in China

THE HAPPY PRINCE

A Tale by
OSCAR WILDE

illustrated and adapted by
MAISIE PARADISE SHEARRING

 Thames & Hudson

High above the city stood the statue of
the Happy Prince. He was a beautiful statue,
covered with fine leaves of gold, with two
bright sapphires for eyes and a large ruby
on the hilt of his sword. People came from
far and wide to see the Happy Prince.

One night, a Swallow arrived in the city.
He was on his way to Egypt to meet his friends.

He decided to rest on the feet of the statue.

The Swallow was very happy with his golden perch.
But as he drifted off to sleep, a large drop of water fell on him.
This was odd, because the night sky was clear and warm.

Then another drop fell on him. When the third drop fell, the Swallow wondered if he should find a new place to sleep. Then he looked up.

There were tears running down the statue's face. "Why are you weeping?" the Swallow asked. "I thought you were a Happy Prince."

The Happy Prince spoke. "When I was alive and had a human heart, I lived in a palace just outside the city. I lived a life of luxury."

"I never cried, because I had no reason to cry.
I was happy. I didn't care what happened to my
people. I only cared about my own happiness."

"But now, when I look out at the city, I see sorrow.
Far away in a little street, a seamstress lives with her little boy.
The boy is ill. His mother is sewing a dress for the Queen,
but until she is paid for her work, she can't buy food or
medicine for her poor son."

"Please, little Swallow, take
them the ruby from my sword.
I wish I could take it myself,
but I cannot move."

The Happy Prince looked so sad that the Swallow agreed to stay for one more night to help.
Then the Swallow took the ruby and flew over the city, looking for the seamstress and her son.

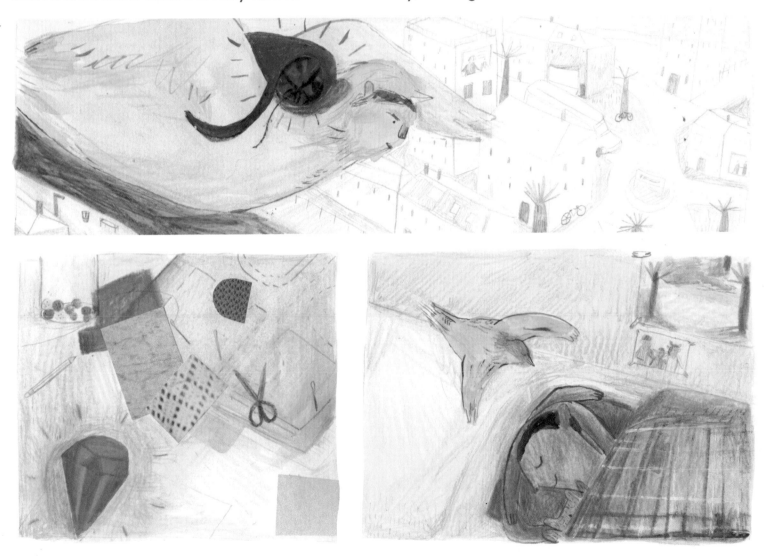

He placed the ruby beside the seamstress and fanned the boy's
face with his wings until the little boy fell into a peaceful slumber.

The next day was cold but the Swallow felt warm.

The Happy Prince said this was because he had done a good deed.

When the moon rose, the Swallow went to say goodbye to the

Happy Prince but the Prince had something else to ask.

"Swallow, Swallow, little Swallow, far away on the other side of the city, I can see a young man in his attic. He is trying to write a play for the stage. He dreams of being a writer but is very cold and cannot afford wood for the fire."

"Happy Prince, I will stay for another
night to help," the Swallow said.
"Shall I take another ruby?"

"Alas, I have no more rubies,"
the Prince said. "All I have left are
my eyes, which are sapphires.
Take one of them and carry it to him."

So the Swallow plucked out one of the Prince's eyes and took it to the young writer's attic.

"This must be from an admirer of my work," the young man thought. "Now I can finish my play!"

The next evening, the Swallow went to say goodbye to the Happy Prince. But the Prince said, "Swallow, Swallow, little Swallow, please stay just one night more."

"But it is winter and the snow will soon be here. In Egypt, it is warm and my friends are enjoying the sun. I have to go."

"Next winter, I will come back with
two beautiful jewels to replace
the ones you gave away."

"In the square below is a little match girl," the Prince said. "All her matches have fallen in the gutter and are spoiled. She is crying because she knows her father will be furious if she does not bring home some money. Take my other eye to her, so her father will not be angry."

"I can stay with you one more night," the Swallow said. "But I cannot take your eye. You would be blind."

But the Happy Prince stood firm. "Swallow, Swallow, little Swallow, please do as I ask."

So the Swallow took the Happy Prince's other eye and flew away.

He found the little match girl and dropped the jewel into the palm of her hand.

She ran home laughing.

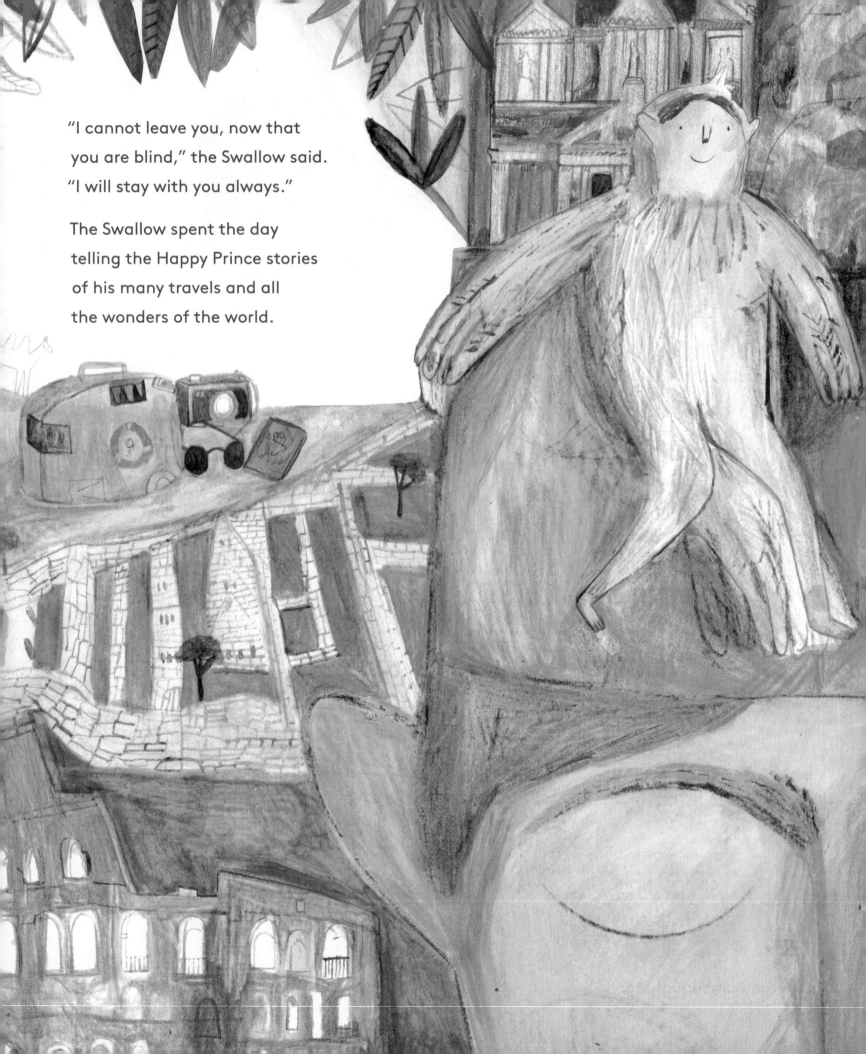

"I cannot leave you, now that you are blind," the Swallow said. "I will stay with you always."

The Swallow spent the day telling the Happy Prince stories of his many travels and all the wonders of the world.

"Dear little Swallow," the Happy Prince said, "you tell me of astonishing things but there is nothing more astonishing than the suffering of men and women. There is no mystery so great as misery. Fly over my city, little Swallow, and tell me what you see there."

So the Swallow flew over the city. He saw rich people and poor people and hungry children.

The Swallow told the Happy Prince what he had seen.

"I am covered with fine gold," the Prince said.

"You must take it off and give it to the poor. Living people
always believe that gold will make them happy."

So the Swallow picked each gold leaf off the Happy Prince
until he was dull and drab, and gave the gold to the poor.
The children's faces grew rosier. They began to laugh
and play games in the street.

Then the snow came.

The Swallow grew colder and colder. But he would not leave the Happy Prince. The Swallow loved him too much.

Finally, the Swallow grew weary and weak.
He knew this day would be his last.

"Goodbye, dear Prince," the Swallow said.
"Will you let me kiss your hand?"

"So you are going to Egypt at last, little Swallow!
You must kiss me on the lips, for I love you."

"I am not going to Egypt but to the house
of Death," the Swallow said, and kissed
the Happy Prince on the lips.

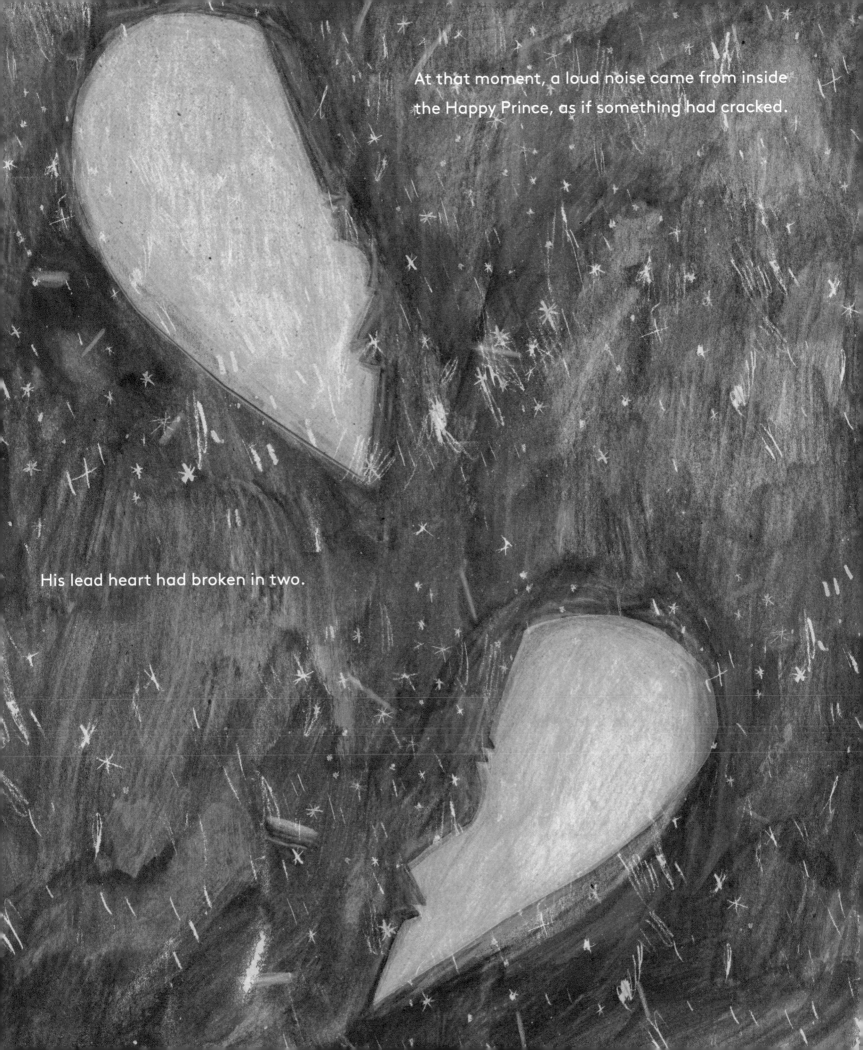

At that moment, a loud noise came from inside the Happy Prince, as if something had cracked.

His lead heart had broken in two.

Early the next morning the Mayor was waiting in the square below. He looked up at the statue: "Dear me! How shabby the Happy Prince looks!" he said. So the Mayor gave the order to pull the statue down.

"He is not beautiful and he is not useful," the Mayor said. The Prince was taken to be melted down.

"How strange," a man said. "This broken lead heart won't melt in the furnace. We'll have to throw it away."

So they threw it on a dust heap where the dead Swallow was also lying.

God sent down an Angel to look for the two most precious things in the city. The Angel chose the Swallow's dead body and the Happy Prince's broken heart of lead.

The Swallow and the Happy Prince were reunited and lived happily together in the garden of Paradise, forever.

Oscar Wilde was born in Dublin in 1854, into a family of intellectuals. He studied at Oxford University and was famed for his sharp wit. He could also speak several languages and had a wide-ranging classical education. He is considered one of the greatest writers of the Victorian era. He wrote nine plays, one novel, and many poems and short stories. In 1888 he published *The Happy Prince and Other Tales*, a collection of stories for children that he wrote for his two sons, Cyril and Vyvyan. He died in Paris on November 30th, 1900, at the age of 46.